The Royal Derby

By Kathy Ellen Davis

Illustrated by the Disney Storybook Art Team

A Random House PICTUREBACK® Book
Random House 🏠 New York

Random House Children's Books supports the First Amendment and celebrates the right to read.

One day, Ms. Featherbon gathered the pets in the Pawlace for a special announcement.

"The Whisker Haven Royal Derby is today," she said. "It's a pony race of splendificent magnificence!"

Ms. Featherbon sprinkled some glitterbits into the birdbath. "One pet will be chosen to be the Royal Derby Starter," she continued. "Look closely, and the chosen pet will appear."

Bum! Bum! Bum!

Lily played a drumroll while everyone peered into the birdbath.

Just then, Treasure burst through the doors of the Pawlace in her sailboat.

It was headed straight for the pets! Treasure swerved and jumped off the boat right before it crashed into a nearby wall.

Boom!

Treasure bounced off Lily's drum . . .

. . . and landed in
Ms. Featherbon's
birdbath!

Ms. Featherbon looked at the soaked kitten. "The birdbath has decided," she announced, "that Treasure is the Royal Derby Starter!"

"What's a Royal Derby Starter?" asked Treasure.

"The starter of the Royal Derby, silly," explained Pumpkin as she helped her friend out of the birdbath. "But first you'll need a hat. Follow me!"

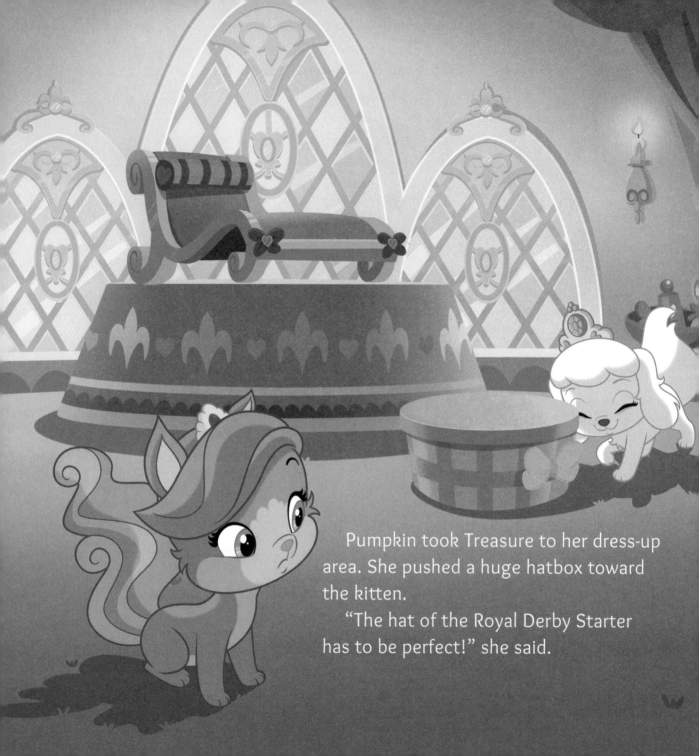

Pumpkin took Treasure to her dress-up area. She pushed a huge hatbox toward the kitten.

"The hat of the Royal Derby Starter has to be perfect!" she said.

Treasure opened the box. She'd always wanted a pirate hat or a knight's helmet.

Instead, she found the frilliest, silliest hat she had ever seen!

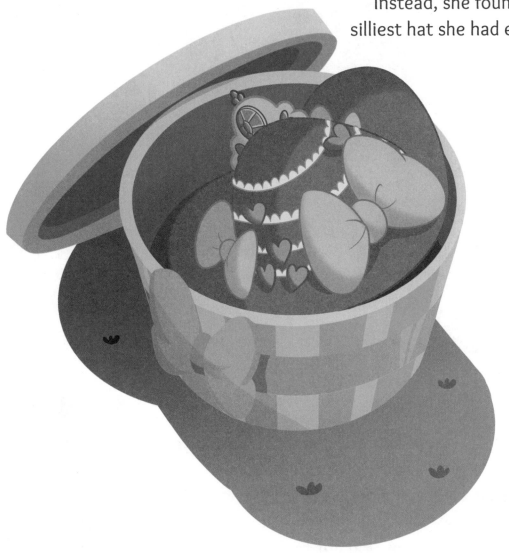

"I made it myself!" Pumpkin said. "What do you think?"
Treasure didn't know what to say.
"Uh . . . it's . . . ," she began.
"Oh, I just love the Whisker Haven Royal Derby!" exclaimed
Pumpkin. "I'm so happy you get to wear my special hat."

Then Pumpkin gave Treasure a big hug.
But Treasure still wasn't sure about wearing
the hat. It was so silly!

Maybe it won't be so bad, thought Treasure as she walked through the Pawlace. After all, Pumpkin had worked really hard on it.

Just then, Sultan popped in and started laughing.

Treasure was embarrassed and angry that she had to wear the silly hat. She stormed away.

But Sultan wasn't laughing at Treasure! He was laughing at one of Berry's jokes. Now he had one for Berry.

"Why do bees have sticky hair?" he asked.

"Because they use honeycombs!" Berry answered.

Sultan wanted to share the joke with Treasure.

But when he turned around, she was already gone.

Meanwhile, down at the track, the ponies were getting ready for the derby.

Treasure was supposed to be at the starting line, but she was worrying about the hat instead.

She was afraid that everyone would laugh at her if she wore it.

If she didn't wear it, no one would laugh at her—but Pumpkin's feelings would be hurt.

Suddenly, it was time to start the derby.

"Are you ready?" asked Ms. Featherbon.

Treasure gulped. She couldn't disappoint Pumpkin, so she climbed up the steps, the hat on her head.

Nothing could prepare her for what she saw next.

All the Critterzens were wearing silly hats. And they were cheering for her!

"What a splendificent hat!" said Ms. Featherbon.

"Thanks!" said Treasure. "It's extra special because Pumpkin made it."

Treasure took a deep breath, then announced:
"Whisker Haven Royal Derby . . . GO!"

The ponies were off! The
Critterzens threw their hats in
the air and cheered.

Treasure cheered, too. But she made sure her hat stayed on her head. She loved it too much to take it off!

"*Hat's* a wrap!" she exclaimed.